MIB
MEN IN BLACK ™

A storybook by Jane B. Mason
Based on the screen story and screenplay by Ed Solomon

Visit the Sony website at
www.sony.com

ISBN 0-590-34415-3

Copyright © 1997 by Columbia Pictures Industries, Inc.
All rights reserved. Published by Scholastic Inc.

12 11 10 9 8 7 6 5 4 3 2   7 8 9/9 0 1 2/0

Designed by Joan Ferrigno

Printed in the U.S.A.   14

First Scholastic printing, June 1997

On a small blue planet, somewhere in our solar system, millions of creatures go about their daily lives. They don't know that alien space creatures are their neighbors, their friends. They don't know about the alien life-forms that live in all parts of outer space. They only know the simple routines of their everyday lives. . . .

It was a dark night in the Texas desert. A boxy black car stood on a lonely stretch of highway. Nearby, the cars of several Immigration and Naturalization Services agents blocked the road.

Huddled in the middle of the road was a group of people who'd been caught trying to enter the United States illegally.

Two men in plain black suits moved through the line of people. One of them spoke in a friendly voice in Spanish, welcoming them to the United States and telling them not to worry.

But when he stepped up to the last man in line, his kind words disappeared. "What are you doing here?" he asked, still speaking Spanish.

The man in line smiled and nodded, pretending to understand.

"You don't understand a word of Spanish, do you?" Again, the man smiled and nodded.

The man in the suit grabbed the illegal immigrant by the arm. "What're we thinking, Dee?" the man asked his partner.

"Tough call, Kay," replied Dee.

"Well, I think we've got a winner here," Kay said. "The rest of you are free to go." Kay and Dee led the man off the road and over a hill.

When they were out of view, Kay pulled a small laser device out of his jacket pocket. "I'll bet dollars to *pesos* that you're not from anywhere *near* here."

BZZZZ! Kay zipped the laser down the front of the man's clothes. The clothes fell to the ground, revealing a scaly space creature!

"Put up your hands," Kay ordered.

Just then a terrified scream rang through the dark night. Standing on the hill, looking right at them, was one of the INS agents from the highway.

"SCREEEEEEEE!" The alien broke free and ran toward the INS agent. He leaped through the air, jaws wide open, knocking Kay's weapon out of his hands.

"Shoot him, Dee," Kay shouted.

Dee fumbled. He couldn't do it. He was frozen. Kay picked up his weapon and fired. There was a blinding flash, and the space creature exploded in a fountain of blue goo that splattered everywhere, including on the INS agent's face.

The agent looked at Kay with wide eyes. "Th-that was — wasn't —"

"Human. I know," Kay replied. "Whoops. Got some entrails on you." He handed the agent a handkerchief.

The agent looked at the disgusting blue mess. He looked up at the sky. He looked at Kay and Dee.

"Who are you?" he asked.

"Just a figment of your imagination." Kay pulled a round metal device from his pocket and held it up.

Curious, the agent peered at it closely.

FLASH! A bright white light glared against the agent's eyeballs. Now he had no memory of the exploding alien. He stared at Kay, confused.

"Hey," he said in a dazed voice. "Where am I?"

Once the agent was gone, Dee sat down on a rock and stared up at the sky. "I'm sorry about what happened back there."

"It happens," Kay said.

Dee held his hands out in front of him. They wouldn't stop shaking. "It didn't used to. I'm going to miss this job, Kay."

"No, you won't, Dee. You won't remember anything about it." Once again, Kay pulled the small metal device from his pocket. This time he erased Dee's memory.

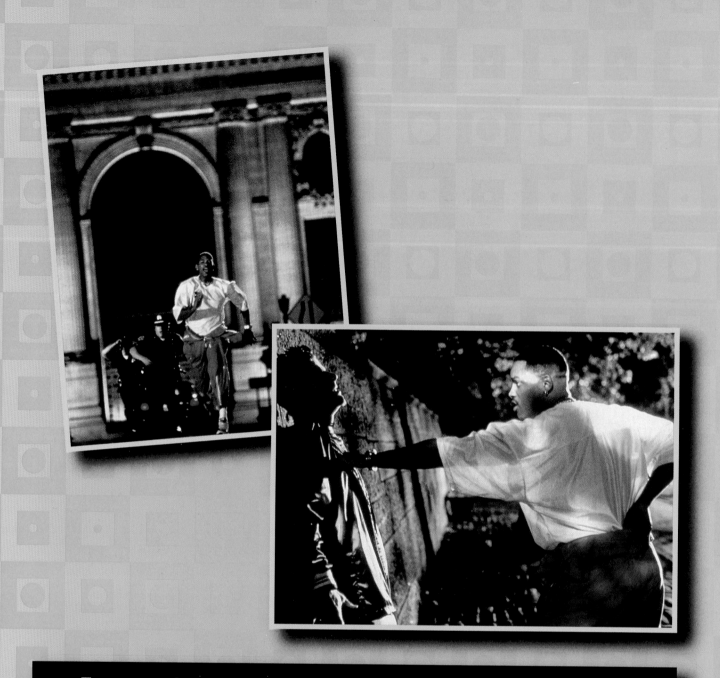

Far away from Texas, in New York City, James Edwards was on a chase. Edwards, an undercover cop, was used to chasing criminals. But this guy was fast.

"Stop!" Edwards shouted. "NYPD!"

The criminal raced onto a bridge. Swinging a leg over the guardrail, he leaped to the street below.

Edwards shook his head in surprise. That was a thirty-foot drop! He hurdled over the guardrail himself just in time to see the criminal making his getaway.

Edwards caught up to the criminal and tackled him. But before he could get the handcuffs on, the criminal pulled out a strange-looking weapon. Edwards knocked it away... and it shattered into a million pieces!

"What the —?"

The distraction was all the criminal needed. Scrambling to his feet, he leaped twenty feet up to a landing on the roof of a nearby building!

Edwards couldn't believe it. Who *was* this guy?

Edwards bolted into the building and raced to the roof. Kicking open a door, he caught the criminal by surprise.

The criminal backed to the edge of the roof. "He's coming because I failed! Your world is gonna end!"

Perched at the edge of the roof, the criminal blinked. Not once, but twice — with *two* sets of eyelids!

"What *are* you?" Edwards demanded.

But the criminal didn't answer. Instead, he leaped off the building to his death.

A few hours later, Edwards was sitting in the police station answering questions. He felt totally frustrated. No one believed his story!

Then, a man in a plain black suit stepped into the room. "Those weren't eyelids," he said. "They were gills. Did he say anything to you?"

"Yeah, sure," Edwards said sarcastically. "He said the world is coming to an end."

"Would you recognize his weapon if you saw it again?"

Edwards nodded. "Absolutely."

"Let's take a ride."

Soon Edwards and the man were pulling up in front of Jeebs's pawnshop.

"Believe me, Jack Jeebs doesn't *sell* what I saw," Edwards objected.

The man in the suit ignored him as they stepped into the store. A sleazy-looking man was behind the counter.

"Show him the imports, Jeebs."

"H-hiya, Kay," Jeebs said nervously. "How are you?"

Kay pointed his weapon at Jeebs's head. "The imports, Jeebs. I'm counting to three. One . . . two . . . three . . ."

KA-BOOM! Jeebs fell to the floor in a heap.

Edwards gasped. This Kay guy was a lunatic!

"Don't *do* that," said an irritated voice. "Do you know how much that hurts?"

Edwards whirled around. Jeebs was growing a new head!

Jeebs pushed a button and the counter flipped over, revealing a shelf piled with space alien weapons.

Edwards pointed to one of them. "Uh, this," he said in a dazed voice. "This is what I saw."

A few minutes later Edwards and Kay left the pawnshop. Edwards felt like he was dreaming. "The eyelids, fine...and the jumping thing...and the gun. But the head? A head doesn't grow back." He looked at Kay. "What's going on?"

Hesitating, Kay pulled his neuralyzer out of his pocket. He hated to do it, but he'd have to erase Edwards's memory.

Well, maybe he could make it up to him later. Get him to join the Men in Black. It wouldn't be easy. Edwards would have to pass a series of tests. And he might not want to work for the agency. But Kay had a feeling that James Edwards had what it took.

In upstate New York, a strange light was hovering over a small farm. It got bigger and bigger, glowing bright red.

WHAM! The light slammed into a truck parked outside the farmhouse. Flames and smoke shot into the dark sky.

Seconds later a burly man named Edgar threw open the farmhouse door. Clutching his shotgun, Edgar walked toward what used to be his truck. Now it was just a shell with a giant hole.

Edgar peered into the hole and blinked. It went ten feet down! Embedded in the ground was a shiny metal spaceship, complete with blinking lights.

A long, hairy pincer flashed out of the hole, grabbed Edgar by the head, and pulled him down into it.

R-I-I-I-P-P! Glug. Glug. Glug. Something sailed out of the hole and landed on the ground with a thump. It was Edgar. At least, it looked like Edgar.

Minutes later, Edgar walked back into his kitchen. "Sugar," he said to his wife. "Give me water, with sugar in it."

Beatrice looked at her husband in alarm. "Edgar, your skin! It's hanging off of your bones."

Edgar checked his reflection in a window. Twisting his face around, he tucked his neck skin into his shirt collar.

"That better?" he said with a grin.

The following morning, Edwards went into a building in downtown Manhattan. There he competed with several other young men. But only one would become a new member of the Men in Black. Edwards took a series of tests and proved he was the best. Kay asked him to become his partner.

"Back in the mid-fifties, the government started an agency to make contact with aliens," Kay said. He was showing Edwards around agency headquarters. "Everyone thought it was a joke. But aliens made contact on March 2, 1961." He handed Edwards a photograph of a flying saucer.

Then Kay showed Edwards another photo, this one of the 1964 World's Fair grounds in New York City. Two giant spires topped with flying saucers towered over everything else.

"They landed at the World's Fair?" Edwards was shocked.

Kay nodded. "They were looking for a place to live in peace. Nonhumans still arrive every day. They live among us, in secret."

Edwards raised an eyebrow. In spite of everything he'd seen, he didn't believe a word Kay was saying. Did he *want* to become this man's partner?

Then Kay opened an unmarked door, and Edwards's jaw dropped. A group of tall, skinny, wormlike aliens were standing around a coffee machine, chatting in a strange language.

Edwards took a deep breath. Kay was telling the truth!

The next day, James Edwards was sworn into the agency. His fingerprints were erased. His driver's license and credit cards were taken away. His name was changed. From now on, he was simply Jay.

Jay got a new black suit. Some black sunglasses. And a pair of shiny black shoes.

He was one of them now: the Men in Black.

That afternoon, Jay and Kay got their first assignment as a team. An alien named Redgick had left Manhattan without permission. It was their job to bring him back.

When they pulled the alien's car off the highway, Kay was surprised to find Mrs. Redgick clutching her swollen belly. She was going to have a baby any minute!

"Okay. No big deal," Kay said. He turned to Jay. "You handle it. You just sorta...catch." He gave Jay a supportive slap on the back and pulled Redgick aside.

"Your wife's doctor is back in Manhattan. You were headed out of town."

Redgick looked a little nervous. "Well, uh, we had to get out of our neighborhood. We don't like the new arrivals."

"What new arrivals?" Kay asked. He remembered hearing about a recent unauthorized landing upstate. "Does this have anything to do with the illegal ship that landed last night?"

Meanwhile, Jay was wiping his brow. This wasn't easy!

"Guys!" Jay gasped. "Helllpppp!" The next thing he knew, he was lying in the dirt with a multitentacled alien baby on his chest.

Kay gave Redgick a slap on the back. "Congratulations!" he crowed. "It's a squid!"

Jay looked up at the creature on his stomach and smiled. "Hey, you know, it *is* sorta . . ."

BLAHHHH! The baby threw up right in Jay's face.

"Something about that was strange," Kay said when they were back in the car. "We should check the hot sheets."

Jay shot his partner a look. What about their assignment *wasn't* strange?

Kay pulled over at a newsstand and started riffling through the tabloid newspapers.

"*These* are the hot sheets?" Jay couldn't believe it.

"Best investigative reporting in the country," Kay replied. "There it is." He smacked the paper down with the pages open to a huge headline: "ALIEN STOLE MY HUSBAND'S SKIN!"

It didn't take Jay and Kay long to find Edgar's wife, and she was thrilled to tell her story.

"I know Edgar," Beatrice said. "And whoever came back into the house wasn't him. It was more like something *else* that was *wearing* him. Like a suit. An Edgar suit."

"Did he say anything?"

"He asked for water. Sugar water."

Kay pulled out his neuralyzer. FLASH! Beatrice froze, as if she were hypnotized. She wouldn't remember a thing.

Minutes later, Kay was using a special analyzer to find out what kind of alien had landed. He held the little machine above some alien tracks. The analyzer changed colors, from red to yellow. "Please, not green," Kay said. Yellow to purple. Purple to green.

Kay moaned. Only one kind of alien left a green trail. He contacted Zed, his boss, back at headquarters.

"We got a Bug on our hands," Kay said. "They infest and destroy. We'd better keep an eye on the morgues."

Back in New York City, a roundish man carrying a cat and a carved wooden box walked into a Russian diner. After scanning the dining room, he approached a tall, dignified-looking man sitting alone. The two embraced awkwardly and sat down at a small table.

The tall man raised his glass of wine in a toast. "To peace." They clinked glasses and drank.

"To think that after all these years of war," the tall man said, "we'd meet in a stink hole like this."

The other man shrugged. "Earth? It's not so bad once you get used to the smell."

In the kitchen, a Russian cook slapped an order onto the stainless-steel counter. "Table six is up!" he called.

A pair of hands reached over, picked up the plates, and carried them into the dining room.

When the waiter arrived at the table, the man with the wooden box froze in fear. This wasn't the waiter who had taken their order. It was Edgar — the alien Bug. "You can kill us both, but it will not stop the peace," the man said.

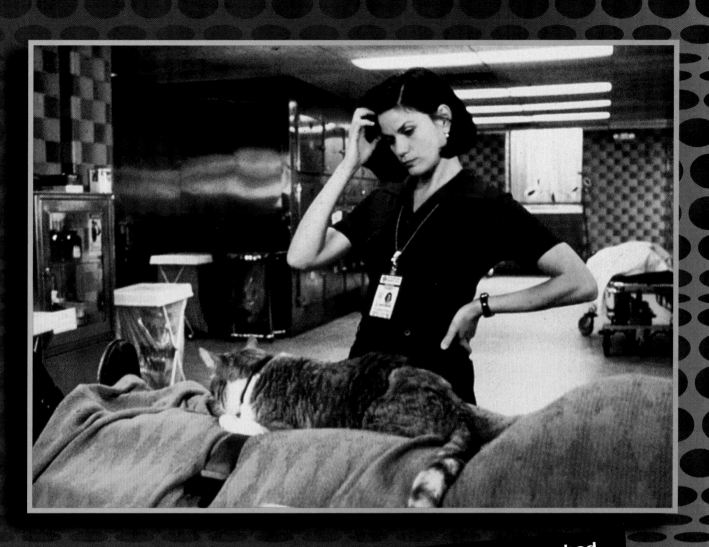

Edgar didn't reply. A long, slender stinger reached out from under the back of his apron and slid under the table. A second later, both men lurched and fell forward, dead.

Edgar moved quickly, searching the men's pockets. But he couldn't find what he was looking for. Soon other customers were looking his way. Someone screamed.

Edgar tried to pry open the wooden box, but it was locked. Shoving it under his arm, he bolted for the door. The man's cat jumped up on the table and hissed at Edgar as he ran out of the restaurant.

A little while later, the bodies from the Russian diner arrived at the city morgue. Jay and Kay weren't far behind. They burst into the room, pretending to be doctors.

The medical examiner, Dr. Laurel Weaver, met them at the door.

"You've got something unusual?" Kay asked.

Laurel pulled back a sheet, revealing the tall man from the diner. Only now that he was dissected, you could see that he wasn't a man. He was an alien, an Arquillian.

Jay steadied himself as he looked at the gruesome sight. But Kay stepped forward, excited. "I'll have a look at this one," he said. "Why don't you two check out the other body?"

"Meowww." Jay looked down as a large cat rubbed against his leg. "Your cat?" he asked.

"I guess it is now," Laurel replied. "It came in with the bodies." She snapped on rubber gloves and started to dig around inside the corpse.

Trying not to think about it, Jay did the same.

"Feel anything strange?" Laurel asked. "Stomach? Liver? Lungs?"

"Nope. All fine," Jay replied.

"Doctor! They're all *missing*." She leaned in close to Jay's ear. "I don't think this is a body at all, but a transport unit for something else altogether. The question is: what?"

She pulled her hand out of the corpse and began to examine its head. Her eyes widened as she noticed some strange stitching around its ear.

Curious, Jay reached out and touched it. The ear turned easily in his hand. With a soft click, it pulled away from the head like a latch. Then the whole face opened up like the top of a box.

Sitting inside the empty skull was a tiny green man surrounded by gears, controls, and viewing screens!

"Far *out*!" Laurel exclaimed.

But the little green man was seriously wounded. "Must to pre—prevent . . ." He searched for the right word. "Contest? No . . ."

"It's all right," Jay said soothingly. "What are you trying to say? Struggle?"

"War?" Laurel suggested.

The little green man nodded. "Galaxy on or—or—Orion's . . ." He thought for a second. "Be . . ."

"Bed? Belt?" Jay was excited now. "Orion's Belt?"

The little green man nodded again. Then he fell over and died.

Kay came over to the corpse on the table. "Rosenberg," he said sadly. "One of the few I actually liked."

"I was right!" Laurel said. "This is an alien life-form, and you're from some government agency that wants to keep it under wraps . . ."

Without hesitating, Kay pulled his neuralyzer from his pocket. FLASH!

"The little man said, 'To prevent war, the galaxy is on Orion's Belt,'" Jay said. He looked up at Laurel's blank face.

"Oh, man, you did the flashy thing already," Jay complained. "It'll probably give her brain cancer!"

Meanwhile, Edgar was in a stolen van, desperately trying to open the carved wooden box. Growling with rage, he hurled the box against the van door. CRACK! One of the hinges broke off. Edgar snapped it up and pried away the rest of the hinge. Then he pulled off the lid.

Inside, thousands of precious diamonds glittered in the light. With an angry snort, Edgar tossed them aside.

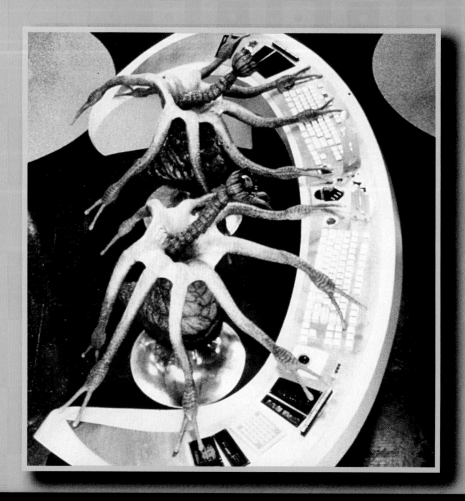

By now the sun was coming up over the Manhattan sky-scrapers. At Men in Black headquarters, workers were busily manning computers and monitoring aliens on Earth.

Jay rubbed his eyes. "Doesn't anybody believe in sleep around here?"

"We're on Centaurian time," Kay's boss, Zed, replied. "A thirty-seven-hour day." They stepped up to a large screen. "Here's Orion, the brightest grouping of stars in the northern sky. But there are no galaxies on Orion's Belt. The belt is just three stars. Galaxies have *billions*."

Kay looked at the screen that showed aliens on Earth. "They're leaving." He sounded concerned. "Show us a four-thousand-field view of Manhattan," he said.

The image on the screen changed to show Earth from outer space. But Earth wasn't the only thing in the picture. An alien battle cruiser hovered nearby, ready to fight.

"That's an Arquillian battle cruiser," Kay said with a sigh. "And we just saw a dead Arquillian ambassador."

"Get down to Rosenberg's shop and see what you can turn up," Zed instructed. "And take a lot of fire power."

SMASH! The glass door to Rosenberg's jewelry shop shattered into a million pieces. A fleshy gray hand reached in and fumbled with the locks. A moment later, Edgar stepped inside.

Jewels of every color glittered under the glass cases. One by one, Edgar smashed them all. Grabbing handfuls of jewels, he tossed them aside in disgust.

The roar of an engine made Edgar look up. His van was being lifted onto a tow truck!

Edgar thundered outside. "That's my van!" he shouted. He was so distracted he didn't see Jay and Kay walk into the jewelry shop.

Jay eyed the shattered jewelry cases. "Who robs a jewelry store and leaves the jewels?"

"Someone who's not looking for jewels," Kay replied.

A movement outside the store caught Jay's attention. "The Bug in the Edgar suit! It's him!" Jay shouted. He sprinted out the door just as Edgar hopped into the tow truck and gunned the engine. Jay fired, separating the tow truck from the van. The tow truck sped up. Jay leaped onto a parked car and aimed his weapon. But as Edgar turned a corner, a huge truck backed into his line of fire. PKROOWW! The truck exploded and Jay was hurled backward.

When he looked up, Kay was standing over him. "We do not fire our weapons in front of civilians," he said.

"Can we drop the cover-up? An alien battle cruiser is about to blow up the world if we don't . . ."

"There's *always* a battle cruiser, or an intergalactic plague, or *something* about to wipe out life on this planet. The only thing that lets people get on with their lives is that *they don't know about it!*"

Feeling sheepish, Jay looked around. The streets were a mess. Smoking rubble was everywhere. Flocks of people had stopped to stare.

"Just a little swamp gas, folks," he assured them meekly. "Nothing to worry about."

Edgar was pacing the streets of New York. He grabbed a news vendor by the collar. "Where do you keep your dead?" he bellowed. The man gasped for air. "The city morgue!"

As Edgar shoved him away, something caught his eye. It was a postcard display, labeled NEW YORK CITY LANDMARKS. Fascinated, Edgar picked up one of the postcards. He shoved it into his pocket and hurried off.

Kay's black car screeched to a halt in front of a hardware kiosk in lower Manhattan. Kay was in a hurry. Aliens were leaving the planet as fast as you could count. The Arquillian battleship had sent a threatening message. And a second battle cruiser—one belonging to the little green man's people—had parked itself on the other side of Earth.

The only good news was that Edgar's ship was at Men in Black headquarters. Without it, he couldn't leave Earth.

A man in a grubby sweater was closing up the hardware kiosk while his dog waited patiently. Jay glanced at the vendor. "Of course that guy's an alien. That's the worst disguise I've ever seen."

"You should talk, mister. You're not so great-looking yourself."

Jay looked around. The dog was talking!

"Closing early, Frank?" Kay said to the dog.

Frank wagged his tail. "Sorry, Kay, I can't talk right now. My ride's leaving in —"

Kay scooped Frank into his arms. "Call the pound. We got a stray," he shouted.

"Hey! Get your paws off me!" Frank growled.

Kay got right to the point. "Arquillians and Baltians. What do you know?"

"I know they've been fighting since forever over a third galaxy. The Baltians were going to turn over the galaxy. But the Bug had other plans."

"Rosenberg mentioned 'Orion's Belt.' What did he mean?"

"Beats me," Frank said. "I heard the galaxy was here."

"Millions of stars and planets?" Jay said. "Impossible."

"You humans just don't get it," Frank said. "Just 'cause something's important doesn't mean it's not very, very small. The size of a marble. Or a jewel." He squirmed in Kay's arms. "Now if you'll excuse me, I need to be walked before the flight."

Kay dropped Frank and turned to his partner.

"The little green dude was trying to say something before he died," Jay said. "I thought it was 'belt,' but his English wasn't so good."

"Maybe he meant something else," Kay suggested.

The two men thought hard for a minute. A marble. A jewel.

"Hey," Jay said suddenly. "Maybe he meant..."

At the morgue, Laurel was trying to get some work done. The problem was, Rosenberg's cat kept jumping onto the files she was studying.

"Boy, you like attention." Laurel reached out to pet the cat and its jeweled collar caught her eye. The word "Orion" was written across it. "That's a pretty name," Laurel murmured.

Outside, the doorbell rang. But Laurel was distracted by a circular object dangling from the cat's collar. It was made of an odd but beautiful metal, with a light-green center.

"What's this?" Laurel said, peering into the stone. Her eyes widened in amazement as she felt herself being pulled into the stone. For a moment, she sailed through a beautiful starfield with millions of stars and planets.

Laurel sat back in her chair, dazed. "Wow."

The doorbell rang again, and Orion snarled. Leaping off the desk, the cat disappeared under some lab equipment.

Kay and Jay drove the LTD to the morgue.

"So two species have been fighting over a galaxy for years, and the only people who've been benefiting are a race called 'Bugs.' Now the first two species want to make peace, and the Bugs have sent Edgar down to make sure that *never* happens."

"By killing the peacemakers and stealing the galaxy," Kay added. "Right."

"And if we don't get it back before he leaves the planet, we're history."

"Not even history," Kay said. "Because nobody will be around to remember us."

Edgar burst into the morgue. "Where's the animal?" he demanded.

But before Laurel could answer, a bell in the hallway rang. "Hello?" a voice called.

Edgar put a decaying finger to his lips. "Shhhh."

A minute later, Jay came into the morgue. "I'm Sergeant Friday," he said. "I'm looking for the cat that came in with a corpse the other day."

"I don't know where the cat is at the moment," Laurel replied. Then she dropped her voice to a whisper. "Maybe you'd like to take me with you instead."

Jay stepped back, surprised. Laurel must *really* like him.

"I have something I need to show you." She pointed to the examination table in front of her.

Jay tilted his head, confused.

Laurel sighed in frustration. "There's something that *you* have to *help* me with."

Jay's jaw dropped as he realized what was going on. Someone was hiding under the table! He reached for his gun just as Kay came through the door.

But Edgar was too fast. He burst out from under the exam table and threw an arm around Laurel's neck.

HISSS! Orion leaped from her hiding place onto Edgar's back. Edgar grabbed the cat, pulled the little galaxy stone from its collar, and flung the animal across the room.

"REEOOWWW!" Orion screeched as her collar ripped free.

Opening his mouth, Edgar gulped down the galaxy. "Drop your weapons," he said. "We're leaving."

"Without your ship?" Kay prodded.

Edgar didn't answer. With a tight hold on Laurel he escaped through an airshaft. On the street, he yanked a cabdriver from his car seat.

Edgar pushed Laurel behind the wheel and shoved the postcard he'd taken from the newsstand in front of her face. "Take me *here*," he demanded.

Jay and Kay raced back to Men in Black headquarters. But when they got there, there was no sign of Edgar.

"Maybe he's not coming," Jay said.

"There's no other way off the planet!" Kay replied.

Just then an alarm bell rang. The Arquillian ship had fired at the Baltians. Then the Baltians fired back. And Earth was right in between!

"What are they shooting at us for?" Jay asked in a panic. "Can't they settle this in their own galaxy?"

"The treaty requires them to meet in a part of the universe that has no intelligent life-forms," Zed explained.

"You're talking about *us*!" Jay said, stunned. Turning away, a mural caught his eye. It pictured the World's Fair grounds in Queens — the one with the two flying saucers.

"Uh, old guys?" Jay pointed to the flying saucers on the mural. "Do those still work?"

A yellow taxi peeled to a stop outside the fairgrounds. Edgar's postcard sat on the dashboard, showing a picture of the grounds — and the flying saucers.

"You're coming with me," Edgar said, shoving Laurel out the door. He dragged her to the towers and started to climb, pushing her ahead. "It's a long trip. I'll need a snack."

Desperate, Laurel kicked Edgar squarely in the face. He lost his grip for a second, and she flung herself into the air.

THUNK! Laurel landed in the branches of a tree, high above the ground. She hung on for dear life.

SCREEECHHH! A boxy black car halted outside the fairgrounds. Kay and Jay scrambled out, but they were too late. One of the flying saucers was already humming. Spinning faster and faster, it rose into the air.

Kay raised his weapon. "Press the green button on three." Jay took aim.

"One . . . two . . . three." Kay and Jay pulled their triggers.

WHUMP! A giant shock wave rolled out from the gun barre Jay and Kay were sucked to the earth like magnets to refrigerator.

Up in the sky, the shock wave hit the ship — and sucked back to Earth! The flying saucer crashed to the ground. Th hatch opened, and Edgar emerged.

"Move away from the vehicle and put your hands on you head," Jay ordered.

"My hands on my head?" Edgar asked. Then his giant pincer ripped free of the Edgar-arms. The skin on his legs cracke open. And Edgar's head burst like a balloon!

Towering over them was a giant, hairy insect! Its scaly tail ended in a deadly stinger. Two oval eyes stuck out from its snakelike head. And its giant pincers reached twelve feet across!

The Bug raised its pincers into the air, resting them on its head. "Like this?" it asked. And then a wad of slimy brown goo flew from its mouth.

SPLAT! Before Jay and Kay could react, the goo engulfed their weapons and pulled them into the Bug's mouth. It swallowed them in one gulp. Then it swiped at the two men, sending them flying into the air.

"This guy is really beginning to bug me," Kay grunted as he and Jay hit the ground. "Hey, Bug!" Kay shouted, getting to his feet. "You know how many of your kind I've swatted with a newspaper? You're just a smear on the sports page to me, you slimy parasite!"

With a deafening hiss, the Bug cranked open its oozing jaws and sucked Kay into its mouth.

Jay watched in horror as the Bug stretched itself to its full height and howled in triumph. Kay was gone!

But what was that in the Bug's stomach? Jay could make out the shape of two guns...and a human hand reaching for one of them. Kay!

All of a sudden, Jay knew what to do. "Hey!" he shouted at the Bug. "Come over here and try that!"

The Bug ignored him, heading straight for the tower and the second flying saucer.

"What are you, afraid of me?" Jay taunted. "Stand and fight like an anthropoid!" He leaped through the air, landing on the Bug's back.

The Bug shook him off, and Jay landed next to a garbage Dumpster. Getting to his feet, he noticed a cockroach on his sleeve . . . and a hundred more crawling around on the ground.

Stepping forward, he squashed one under his shoe. "I think that was a cousin of yours," Jay yelled to the Bug. Jay stepped on another one. CRUNCH! "That *had* to hurt!"

The Bug turned toward Jay, anger burning in its eyes.

"There's a pretty one!" Jay called. "I know who it is!"

The Bug loomed over him, its jaws dripping.

Jay could see Kay's hand closing around the trigger of the shotgun. He smiled up at the Bug. "It's your momma!"

BLAM! Kay shot a hole through the Bug's abdomen, sending a spray of Bug juice everywhere. The Bug split in two and Kay fell out in a mess of goo. The beautiful green stone dropped to the ground at Jay's feet. Kay picked it up.

Kay reached for his phone and pressed a button. "Get a message to the Arquillians," he told Zed. "We have the galaxy."

A moment later, the Bug raised its head again. HISSS! It attacked, swatting its ugly pincers at Jay and Kay.

BOOM! A shot rang out. The Bug's head exploded into a million bits.

"What the — ?" Jay said.

Laurel stepped out from behind some trees, holding the second weapon that had flown out of the Bug's gut. "Interesting job you guys got," she said.

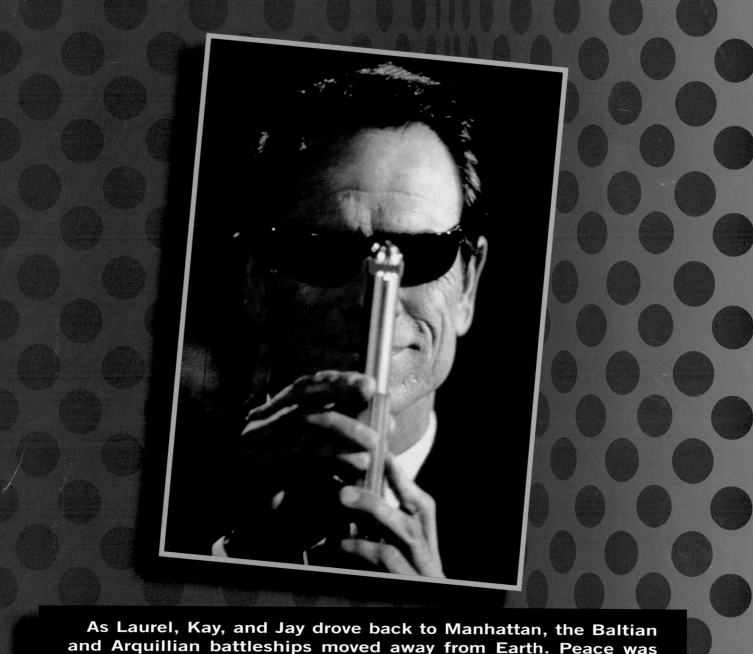

As Laurel, Kay, and Jay drove back to Manhattan, the Baltian and Arquillian battleships moved away from Earth. Peace was restored. Everyone was safe.

When they got back to MiB headquarters, Jay pulled Kay out of the car. Kay took out his memory neuralyzer.

"Don't do it to her again," Jay said to Kay. "Who's she going to tell, anyway? She only hangs out with dead people."

"Not her. Me," Kay said.

"I can't do this job alone."

Laurel got out of the car and joined them.

"Maybe you won't have to." Kay put his finger over Laurel's name tag, covering all the letters except for the L. Then he handed her a pair of sunglasses.

Jay hesitated for a moment. Then he put on his own sunglasses and took the neuralyzer from Kay.

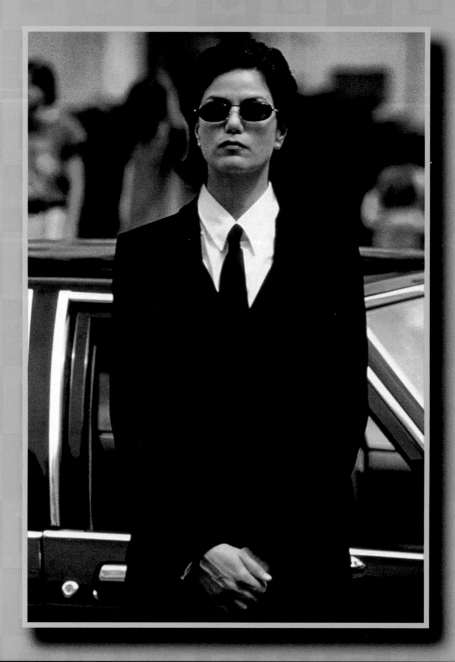

The next afternoon, Jay ran over to the boxy black car with his arms full of newspapers. His new partner, Elle, dressed in a plain black suit, was waiting for him. Together they looked at a picture of a smiling Kay beneath a headline blaring, "MAN AWAKENS FROM THIRTY-YEAR COMA!"
They smiled and climbed into the car.

While human beings go about their daily lives, alien life-forms continue to land on Earth. Most of them only want to live in peace. But others have different plans....